Square Eyes

Written by Karen Tayleur

Illustrated by Gus Gordon

 sundance
A Haights Cross Communications Company

➤ a black dog book

Published by
Sundance Publishing
P.O. Box 1326
234 Taylor Street
Littleton, MA 01460

Copyright © text Karen Tayleur
Copyright © illustrations Gus Gordon

First published 2001 by
Pearson Education Australia Pty. Limited
95 Coventry Street
South Melbourne 3205 Australia
Exclusive United States Distribution: Sundance Publishing

ISBN 0-7608-4984-6

Printed in Canada

Contents

Chapter One

Watching TV _____ 1

Chapter Two

Bang! Sizzle! Broken! _____ 5

Chapter Three

A New Friend _____ 13

Chapter Four

The Perfect Project _____ 23

Chapter Five

A Piece of Cake _____ 31

Characters

Marcus can't stop
watching TV,
and his favorite show
is about cooking.

Tula likes skateboards,
computers,
and having fun.

Chapter One
Watching TV

Marcus Todd had square eyes. Well, he didn't really have square eyes. But he did spend all of his time watching TV. Except, of course, when he was at school. Or in the shower. Or asleep.

His parents said, "Marcus Todd, you will get square eyes if you don't stop watching TV." But Marcus didn't care.

He didn't want to help his mother with her pottery.

He never felt like making model cars with his father.

The boy next door asked Marcus to come out to play. "No thanks," said Marcus. "Maybe later."

That was what he always said. But there never was a later. The boy next door got tired of asking him.

Chapter Two
Bang! Sizzle! Broken!

One night, Marcus climbed out of bed and turned on the TV. He kept the sound down. He sat close to the TV screen. He watched his favorite show.

The TV show was all about cooking.
Creamy soups. Perfect pasta. Amazing
cakes.

Marcus thought the food on TV looked
delicious. He wished his parents could cook
food like that. They both cooked lots of
chicken and boring vegetables.

The next morning, Marcus had trouble getting out of bed. He had stayed up too late watching TV. His brain was too bleary for school. He even fell asleep at his desk.

"Have you finished your worksheet, Marcus?" his teacher asked.

"Half a cup of plain flour," Marcus mumbled. The class laughed.

That afternoon, something terrible
happened. Marcus Todd's TV broke. It
went BANG! Then SIZZLE! Then nothing.

"MOM!" Marcus yelled. His mother rushed into the room. Marcus pointed to the blank TV screen.

"Oh well," said his mother. "That's the end of that." She went back to her pottery.

"DAD!" yelled Marcus.

His father saw the TV and shook his head. "Broken," he said. "Overworked."

"Can you please fix it?" Marcus begged.

But his father had left the room.

"Great," said Marcus. "Now what am I going to do?"

Marcus watched the TV out of habit. He stared at the blank screen until he got bored.

"I'm going to the park," he called to his mom as he went out the door.

Chapter Three
A New Friend

There were plenty of kids at the park. They were all playing games and having fun. Marcus decided to join in. He saw some kids from school flying a kite. He didn't know how to fly a kite.

Some kids were playing tag. Marcus had never played tag in his whole life. He wasn't very good at games. Everything he knew about was on TV.

Marcus Todd sat by himself in the park.
He sat at one end of a seesaw and thought
about the TV show he was missing.

Then WHOOSH! Marcus nearly flew off the seesaw. Up went his seat high into the air. Marcus looked down at the other end of the seesaw. A girl with long, dark hair was sitting there.

"Hi," said the girl.

"Hello," said Marcus.

"You can't do this by yourself," said the girl. She pointed to the seesaw.

"You're right," Marcus said.

Marcus wanted to get off the seesaw. But his feet were high off the ground.

"Isn't it your turn?" said Marcus.

"My turn?" she asked.

Marcus pointed at the ground. The girl laughed and pushed herself up. Slowly, Marcus came down to the ground.

"Thanks," he said. "My name's Marcus Todd. What's your name?"

"Tula. Tula Marika Veradis," she said.
"Mrs. Maxwell's class, Room 8, Dale
Elementary."

She jumped off the seesaw. Then she
grabbed her skateboard and started to walk
away.

"Mrs. Maxwell's class, Room 8?" yelled Marcus. "That's my class."

"Right," Tula agreed.

Marcus didn't know what to say.

"Got to go," said Tula. "Class project, remember?" She kept walking.

"Class project?" he yelled after her. "What class project?"

Marcus ran after Tula. It was hard work because she walked fast. "Tula, wait," he puffed, out of breath.

Tula let him catch up.

Chapter Four
The Perfect Project

"My project's really cool," said Tula. "I've been working on it for ages. Haven't you started? It's due tomorrow."

She put her skateboard on the ground. And gave it a kick with her foot. The skateboard flipped into her hand.

"Maybe you were asleep in class. You do that a lot," said Tula. She set and flipped her skateboard again. "Are you sick or something?"

"No," said Marcus, looking at the skateboard. "I just need lots of sleep."

"My mom knows your mom," said
Tula. "And your mom said that you watch
TV. A lot."

"So?" Marcus felt his face get hot.

"So, your mom told my mom. That's
all." Tula flipped her skateboard. "TV's
okay." She threw him the skateboard. "Do
you want a try?" she said.

Marcus held the skateboard in his hands. He set it on the ground. He kicked at it with his foot like Tula. It flew up and hit him on the leg.

"Ow!" he said. "I've never done this before. It's hard."

"Hey, that's pretty good for your first time," said Tula.

"Anyway," said Tula. "Project. Due tomorrow. I chose surfing."

Marcus set and kicked the skateboard again. He nearly caught it this time.

"What are you going to do?" said Tula.

"I don't even know where to start," said Marcus.

"Do you have any hobbies?" asked Tula.

Marcus tried to think of a hobby—a hobby besides watching TV.

Then Marcus had an idea. "I could do it on cooking," he said.

"What can you cook?" asked Tula.

"Everything," said Marcus. He kicked at the skateboard. It fell over.

"Wow," said Tula. "That's great. I can't cook at all."

Marcus went home. "I've got a project to do," he told his mother. "Could I please use the kitchen?"

His mother looked surprised. "Of course," she said. "But what are you going to do?"

"You'll see," said Marcus.

Chapter Five

A Piece of Cake

Marcus decided to make a cake. He'd seen someone make a cake on TV. It looked pretty easy. He got all of the ingredients and mixed them in a bowl. Then he poured the mixture into a cake pan.

Later, Marcus and his mother pulled a very flat, mushy mess out of the oven.

Marcus phoned Tula. "Something awful has happened," he said.

"What is it?" asked Tula.

"I've just found out I can't cook!" cried Marcus. "Can you help?"

"I'll be right over," said Tula.

Marcus was waiting at the kitchen table when Tula arrived.

"Where's your cookbook?" she asked.

"You need a book?" asked Marcus. "Can't you just tell me what to do?"

Tula laughed. "I can't cook, remember," she said. "You need a recipe from a cookbook."

Marcus searched until he found a cookbook. It was propping up one leg of the kitchen table. He started again and followed the recipe. Step by step. Finally, he slid a new cake pan into the oven.

The next morning, the teacher asked Marcus to talk about his project. Marcus opened the lid of a large cardboard box and lifted out a chocolate cake.

It wasn't a perfect cake. A broken piece was stuck on with frosting. But, the whole class thought it was very tasty. And Marcus was very proud.

That night, Marcus Todd went to bed without even once thinking about TV.